QUEASY QUEST

BY TIM COLLINS
AND JAMES LAWRENCE

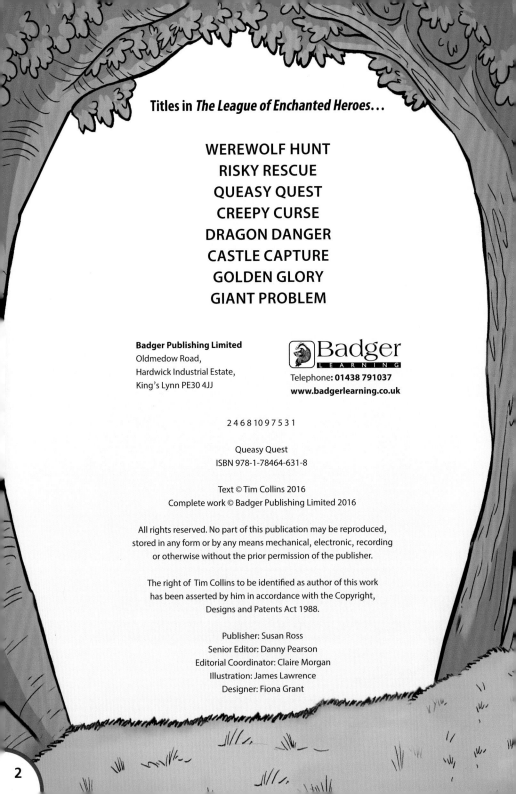

Titles in *The League of Enchanted Heroes…*

WEREWOLF HUNT
RISKY RESCUE
QUEASY QUEST
CREEPY CURSE
DRAGON DANGER
CASTLE CAPTURE
GOLDEN GLORY
GIANT PROBLEM

Badger Publishing Limited
Oldmedow Road,
Hardwick Industrial Estate,
King's Lynn PE30 4JJ

Badger
LEARNING

Telephone**: 01438 791037**
www.badgerlearning.co.uk

2 4 6 8 10 9 7 5 3 1

Queasy Quest
ISBN 978-1-78464-631-8

Text © Tim Collins 2016
Complete work © Badger Publishing Limited 2016

Publisher: Susan Ross
Senior Editor: Danny Pearson
Editorial Coordinator: Claire Morgan
Illustration: James Lawrence
Designer: Fiona Grant

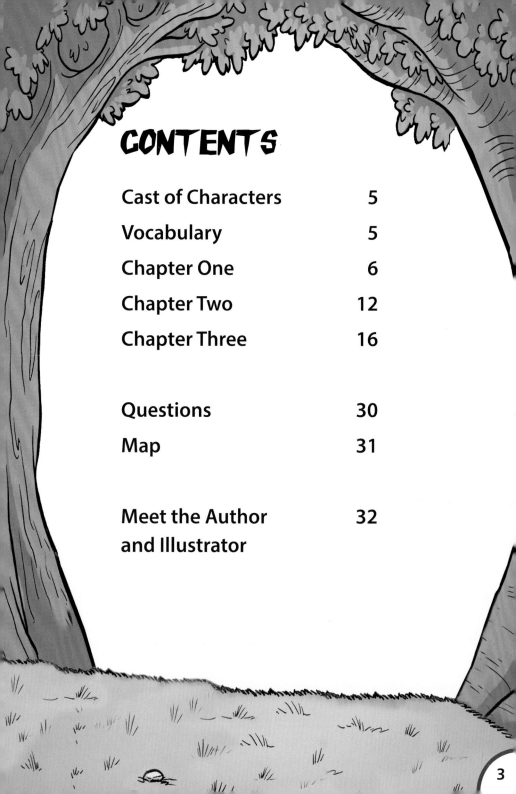

CONTENTS

Jack Mayer used to be an ordinary schoolboy. But when he crossed into Anotherland, he became Jack the Giant Slayer.

Now he's joined the most legendary crime-fighting team ever.

There's Hansel and Gretel with their fearsome magic powers.

Rapunzel, who can battle villains with her strong, long hair.

Red Riding Hood, the world's number one wolf-fighter.

And Tom Thumb, the smallest, toughest, rudest hero around.

Together they're The League of Enchanted Heroes. The bad guys don't stand a chance.

CHARACTERS

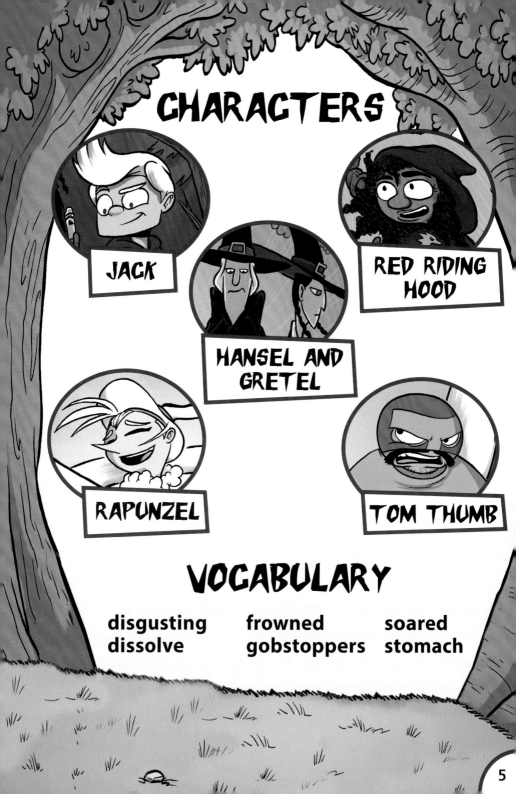

JACK

RED RIDING HOOD

HANSEL AND GRETEL

RAPUNZEL

TOM THUMB

VOCABULARY

disgusting   frowned   soared
dissolve   gobstoppers   stomach

CHAPTER ONE
GIANT MOUTH

Gretel soared above the giant and fired balls of bright blue flame. Hansel shot gobstoppers from his catapult.

The League of Enchanted Heroes had been battling the huge creature for an hour and they had just managed to topple him over.

"Keep the creep on the floor," said Tom Thumb. "I'm going to smash his nose."

Tom Thumb launched himself through the air, aiming for the giant's nose.

At the same time, Hansel fired a gobstopper into the monster's ear.

The giant let out a loud cry, opening his mouth wide.

"No, no, no!" shouted Tom Thumb.

He fell down into the monster's throat, with his arms and legs flapping wildly.

The giant pushed himself to his feet.

He rubbed his stomach and let out a burp that echoed through the forest.

Hansel launched more gobstoppers and Gretel blasted out more flames.

But it was no use. The giant stomped away, shaking the ground with his heavy steps.

CHAPTER TWO
GIANT STOMACH

Tom Thumb slipped down a long pink tube. He tried to grab the sides, but they were coated in slimy spit.

A sharp, strong smell was all around him, making him want to puke.

The tunnel opened out into a large round space.

As he slid into it, he managed to grab hold of a dangling vein.

Tom Thumb swung back and forth over a fizzing pool of stomach acid.

The giant bent forward, shaking Tom Thumb loose. He let go of the vein and tumbled down towards the acid.

"Help!" he cried.

He smacked onto a floating log.

"Can you guys hear me out there?" he yelled. "I'm trapped in this blockhead's stomach and I do not want to use the back exit."

CHAPTER THREE
GIANT SPEW

The giant ran away through the trees.

The others chased after him, scrabbling over thick roots and fallen branches.

"I can hear something inside," shouted Rapunzel.

"Help!" came a muffled voice from deep within the creature.

"Tom Thumb's alive in there," said Red Riding Hood. "We need to get him out as fast as we can!"

Rapunzel sprinted ahead until she was level with the giant.

She leapt onto his foot, tied her hair around his ankle, and jumped off again.

Rapunzel headed into a dense patch of trees, weaving her strong hair between the thick trunks.

The giant tried to lurch onwards, but Rapunzel's hair held fast, and he stumbled down.

"Nooooooooooo!" boomed the giant.

He crashed down to the forest with a loud thud.

"He's stuck," said Red Riding Hood. "Now let's rescue Tom Thumb."

"He'll come out the other end if we wait long enough," said Hansel. "He might not smell too great, but he'll survive."

"No he won't," said Red Riding Hood. "The stomach acid will dissolve him. We need to get him back out of the giant's mouth."

"Let's make him throw up," said Jack. "He'll spew out everything in his stomach, including Tom Thumb."

"Excellent plan," said Red Riding Hood. "Let's all shout out the most disgusting things we can think of."

"Hairy witch warts!" shouted Gretel.

"Steaming dragon droppings!" shouted Hansel.

"Sweaty werewolf armpits!" shouted Red Riding Hood.

"Mouldy school dinner leftovers!" shouted Jack.

The giant grinned, showing his rotten green teeth.

"It's no use," said Gretel. "The giant's so horrible and stinky himself, what could possibly gross him out?"

"That's it!" shouted Jack. "Nasty things are normal to him. So maybe nice things will disgust him."

He turned to the giant and shouted, "Cute kittens!"

The giant frowned. His cheeks turned green and he let out a deep groan.

"It's working," said Red Riding Hood. "Pretty pink flowers!"

"Chocolate boxes!" shouted Hansel.

"Fluffy bunnies!" shouted Gretel.

The giant's mouth flopped open and a thick flood
of puke splurged out.

"Thanks guys," said a voice from inside the creature.

Tom Thumb surfed out on a wave of stinky spew.
He was covered in blobs of sick and splodges of spit.

"I knew you'd rescue me," he said. "You all deserve
a big hug."

"Er... I think we'll pass," said Hansel backing away.

QUESTIONS

Which part of the giant's face was Tom Thumb aiming for? *(page 8)*

What does Tom Thumb land on in the giant's stomach? *(page 14)*

Who uses their hair to trip the giant up? *(page 20)*

What disgusting thing does Red Riding Hood shout about? *(page 24)*

What cute thing does Gretel shout about? *(page 26)*

MEET THE AUTHOR

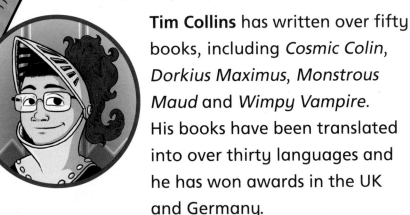

Tim Collins has written over fifty books, including *Cosmic Colin*, *Dorkius Maximus*, *Monstrous Maud* and *Wimpy Vampire*. His books have been translated into over thirty languages and he has won awards in the UK and Germany.

MEET THE ILLUSTRATOR

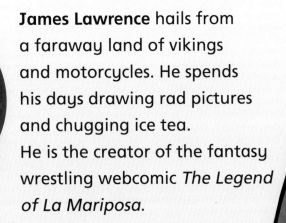

James Lawrence hails from a faraway land of vikings and motorcycles. He spends his days drawing rad pictures and chugging ice tea. He is the creator of the fantasy wrestling webcomic *The Legend of La Mariposa*.